I Don't Want Danny Here

by Elizabeth Dale and John & Gus Art

W
FRANKLIN WATTS
LONDON•SYDNEY

Chapter 1

Izzy really hated tidying up her room.

Why did she have to do it, just because Danny

was coming to stay?

"Hurry up, Izzy," said Dad. "Danny and Julie will be

here soon. You know she's working tonight."

"I don't want Danny to stay here!" Izzy cried.

"Why can't he stay somewhere else while Julie is

at work?"

Dad hugged her. "Izzy, remember Danny's mum

and I are getting married. You like Julie, don't you?"

"Yes, I like *her*," said Izzy. Julie was lovely.

"I'm sure you'll like Danny, too, when you get to know him better," said Dad.

Izzy wasn't so sure about that. Every time Danny came to the house, it went badly. They didn't talk to each other – Danny just sat on the sofa and stared at the floor.

Izzy didn't want him to come and she didn't want to play with him.

Suddenly the doorbell rang.

"They're here!" Dad cried.

5

Chapter 2

Izzy took a long time tidying her bedroom

so she didn't have to go and talk to Danny.

Finally, she went downstairs.

"Hello!" cried Julie, hugging her.

Danny was sitting on the sofa, playing on his tablet. He didn't even look at Izzy.

Izzy followed Dad into the kitchen.

"I'll help you with dinner," she said.

"I'm OK," replied Dad. "You go and talk to Danny.

It's great having everyone together, isn't it?"

Izzy didn't answer — it didn't feel great to her
and she didn't want to tell a lie.

They had sausages for dinner. Izzy loved sausages,
but Danny hardly ate anything and he didn't speak
either. He just glared down at his plate.

"Danny, why don't you show Izzy your remote-controlled car?" said Julie, as they cleared the plates away.

"No!" said Danny, crossly.

"Well, let's play Twister later," suggested Dad.

Playing Twister was good fun. Dad and Julie kept falling over, but Izzy and Danny were brilliant at it.

Then Danny knocked Izzy over.

"Sorry!" he said.

But Izzy was sure he had done it on purpose.

Chapter 3

As soon as Julie left for work, Izzy yawned.

"I'm tired," she said, "I think I'll go to bed."

After a while, Izzy heard Danny come upstairs, too.

Then Dad came in to say goodnight.

"You didn't talk to Danny much tonight," he said.

"He didn't talk to me," Izzy replied, crossly. "I don't

have to like him just because you like his mum."

"Well, please try harder tomorrow," said Dad.
"We will all be living in the same house very soon
and we need to be kind to Danny so that he will
be happy here."

After Dad had gone, Izzy lay there and thought about what he had said.

She liked it when it was just her and Dad.

She knew he was happier now he'd met Julie.

But she wasn't happy. She didn't like Danny.

Izzy couldn't sleep. Finally, she got up to get
a drink. As she passed Danny's room, she heard
a noise. She stopped and listened – Danny was
crying! Izzy tiptoed in.

"What's wrong?" she asked.

"Nothing!" Danny muttered. "Go away."

"Why are you so unhappy?" Izzy asked.

"Why do you think?" Danny snapped.

"I hate coming here. And soon I'll have to move here for good. I am going to lose my home, my school and all my friends."

Suddenly Izzy realised things were going to be even worse for Danny than for her. No wonder he was miserable. Izzy felt bad for not being more friendly.

"I'm sorry," said Izzy. "I thought you just didn't

like me. You don't talk to me and you wouldn't

even let me play with your car."

Danny looked at her. "Girls don't like cars,"

he said.

"Yes they do!" said Izzy. "I like your car."

"Do you want to play with it now?" said Danny, getting out of bed.

"Yes, please," Izzy grinned. "Come on!"

Chapter 4

Danny's car was amazing. It could drive right up the wall – fast!

"It's even better than my robot," said Izzy.

"You've got a robot?" Danny cried. "Can we play
with that, too?"

Izzy showed Danny the tricks her robot could do,
and Danny loved it.

Later, they had a midnight feast and told each other jokes.

"I'm sorry you'll have to leave your friends," Izzy said. "But you can play with my friends at school. You'll like them — they're great. Do you like football?"

"Of course!" Danny said.

Izzy grinned. "So do I. I've got goalposts
in the garage. We could play football tomorrow."

"Great!" smiled Danny. "I think I'll go back to bed
now. I've had fun."

Julie came to pick up Danny straight after breakfast. "Time to go home," she said.

"Oh!" Danny cried. "We wanted to play football. Can I come and stay again soon?"

Julie smiled. "Soon you'll be here every night!" she said.

Danny and Izzy laughed. Living together was going to be strange at first, but maybe it wouldn't be so bad once they got used to it.

Things to think about

1. Why doesn't Izzy like Danny?
2. What happens when they all play a game together?
3. How do you think Danny felt after he pushed Izzy over?
4. Why does Izzy think differently after she hears Danny crying in the night?
5. Do you think Izzy and Danny will like living in the same house after all?

Write it yourself

One of the themes in this story is seeing things from somebody else's point of view. Can you write a story with a similar theme?

Plan your story before you begin to write it.
Start off with a story map:
• a beginning to introduce the characters and where your story is set (the setting);
• a problem which the main characters will need to fix;
• an ending where the problems are resolved.

Get writing! Try to use interesting adjectives, such as miserable, to describe your characters and make your readers understand them.

Notes for parents and carers

Independent reading
This series is designed to provide an opportunity for your child to read independently, for pleasure and enjoyment. These notes are written for you to help your child make the most of this book.

About the book
Izzy's dad is gettting married to Danny's mum. The trouble is that Izzy doesn't like Danny. But when Danny has to stay for the night, and she hears Danny crying, Izzy starts to see things from his point of view.

Before reading
Ask your child why they have selected this book. Look at the title and blurb together. What do they think it will be about? Do they think they will like it?

During reading
Encourage your child to read independently. If they get stuck on a word, remind them that they can sound it out in syllable chunks. They can also read on in the sentence and think about what would make sense.

After reading
Support comprehension and help your child think about the messages in the book that go beyond the story, using the questions on the page opposite.
Give your child a chance to respond to the story, asking:
Did you enjoy the story and why?
Who was your favourite character?
What was your favourite part?
What did you expect to happen at the end?